To Steph

Library of Congress Cataloging-in-Publication Data
Ernst, Lisa Campbell.
    The three spinning fairies: a tale from the
Brothers Grimm/retold by Lisa Campbell Ernst—1st ed.
    p.cm.
    Summary: Three unusual fairies help a lazy girl
try to attain a life of luxury.
    ISBN 0-525-46826-9
    [1. Fairy tales. 2. Folklore—Germany. 3. Laziness—Folklore.]
I. Grimm, Jacob, 1785-1863. II. Grimm, Wilhelm, 1786-1859. III. Title.
PZ8.E7 Th 2002   398.2'0943'01—dc21   2001028536

Published in the United States 2002 by Dutton Children's Books,
a division of Penguin Putnam Books for Young Readers
345 Hudson Street, New York, New York 10014
www.penguinputnam.com

Designed by Lisa Campbell Ernst
Printed in Hong Kong
First Edition
10 9 8 7 6 5 4 3 2 1

The Three Spinning Fairies

A Tale from the Brothers Grimm
retold by Lisa Campbell Ernst

DUTTON CHILDREN'S BOOKS · NEW YORK

ℒong ago, in a kingdom ruled by a persnickety Queen and watched over by three very unusual fairies, there lived a foolish girl named Zelda.

Zelda's poor mother was the Royal Baker. From dawn to dusk she worked until she was ragged, baking delectable pastries to please the finicky Queen. But Zelda refused to help. She fancied herself *much* too special for work of any kind.

No matter what Zelda's mother begged her to do, lazy Zelda had an excuse:

Measure? "Too messy!"

Bake? "Too hot!"

Frost? "Too sticky!"

At last she was assigned the job of spinning the ruby-colored yarn that the Queen ordered to be tied around each royal pastry box. But Zelda whined and complained until her mother ended up doing *that* job as well. "Work is soooooooooo boring," Zelda sighed smugly. And so she sat, day after day, as cozy as one of the Queen's fat cats.

Then one morning, the Queen ordered a five-layer prune cake for a last-minute picnic with the Prince. The bakers were frantic, trying to complete the impossible task. They all feared the Queen's nasty temper—and her dungeon.

Just as royal footsteps were heard outside, the workers rushed to lower the finished cake into its box—but there was no royal yarn to tie around it!

"Quick, Zelda!" her mother whispered.
"Spin us a bit of yarn!"

At that request, Zelda let out an
earsplitting whine that gave shivers
to everyone there—including the
Queen and her dim-witted son, who
had walked in at that very moment.

"*WHAT is going on here?*" the Queen boomed in her high-and-mighty voice.

The kitchen fell deathly quiet, until Zelda's mother slowly stepped forward.

Fearing that Zelda would be punished, her mother lied. "M-m-my daughter is such a hard worker, I simply cannot get her to stop spinning! We argue day and night because we will soon be out of flax!"

The Queen's eyes lit up, and she smiled. "I *love* hard workers, and the sound of spinning is like music to my ears! Let me have your daughter, and she can go on spinning to her heart's content."

Everyone was *thrilled* by this idea. The Queen was looking for a hardworking bride to marry her useless son. The Prince, who cared only about fancy, silly things, thought Zelda looked just his type. Zelda's mother was glad to see Zelda get a job (with someone else). And Zelda thought she would finally have the fancy life she deserved.

The Queen led Zelda to a tower where there were three rooms filled from floor to ceiling with royal flax grown in every color of the rainbow.

"Spin all of this into fine linen thread," ordered the Queen. "When you are done, you may marry my son. I don't mind that you are so poor if you are such a hard worker."

Marry the prince? Hot diggity dog! Zelda nearly fainted with joy. As the door slammed shut, she danced between the piles of flax. Then, looking around, she chuckled to herself. "Queenie can't possibly expect me to work—I'm going to be a princess!"

And for three days she sat, daydreaming of her royal life.

On the third day, the Queen returned. She stared in shock at the untouched flax. No one had ever disobeyed her command.

"What is the meaning of this?" she hissed, her face growing purple with rage.

Zelda began to tremble. "I—I—I was so homesick," she stammered. "I couldn't stop crying long enough to spin."

The Queen eyed her carefully. "Enough!" she snapped.
"Tomorrow I shall expect to see that you have begun your work."
The door closed with a crash and the turn of a key. Now Zelda
began to panic. Never in a million years could she spin all that flax.
She'd be sent to the dungeon—or worse, back to the bakery!
Frantic, Zelda ran to the window to see if she could escape.

Outside, Zelda saw three very strange-looking fairies flying toward her. One had a big flat foot, another's tongue hung out of her mouth, and the third had a huge thumb. They stopped in front of the window.

"What's the problem?" they asked, smiling.

Zelda told the fairies her story.

"Stop whining," they said. "We'd be happy to spin all that flax for you, but here's the deal: we love royal parties, so you must promise to invite us to your wedding, and not be ashamed of us but proudly introduce us as your cousins."

"Sure, sure, anything for a life free from work," said Zelda. "But hurry! The Queen will be back soon."

The fairies introduced themselves as Anita, Benita, and Bob, and they flew straight through the window to begin their work.

Anita used her foot to pump the spinning wheel. Benita used her tongue to moisten the fiber as it was twisted. Bob wound the finely spun thread around his thumb, and each time he hit it on the table, a perfectly shaped skein of yarn fell to the ground.

"Would you like to help, dear?" asked Anita.

"It's great fun," said Benita.

"We could teach you how," added Bob.

Zelda began to laugh. "Gross! The only
thing I hate more than spinning is baking—of course, my mother does
all that! Anyway, I'll never have to work again once I'm a princess."

All day and all night, the fantastic fairies spun.
"You're sure you don't want a turn?" they asked Zelda kindly.
Zelda snorted in reply, turned over, and went back to sleep.

When the Queen came by the next day, Zelda was quick to hide the three workers. Then, with great fanfare, she presented skein after skein of the most finely spun flax.

"Oh, how I do love to *work*!" Zelda crowed every chance she got,
hoping to win her majesty's royal good favor. Zelda's performance was
enough to melt even the iciest Queen—she was tickled pink.

As soon as the first room was empty of the unspun flax, the fairies went on to the second, and then the third. Within another day, all three rooms were nearly filled with spun thread.

One last time, the fairies offered to let Zelda help.

"Forget it," she snapped. "Work is for fools."

And so the amazing fairies finished and said their good-byes.
"Don't forget your promise," Anita warned.
"It will bring you good fortune," Benita added.
"Good-bye for now!" sang Bob, and with that the three fairies
were gone.

When Zelda at last showed the Queen and Prince the three rooms now filled with great piles of thread, they were amazed.

"What a splendid worker!" gasped the Queen, delighted.

"What a beautiful girl!" sighed the Prince, even more delighted.

"What fools!" snickered Zelda, the most delighted of all.

The Queen was true to her word. Raising her scepter, she declared, "I grant you the honor of marrying my son!"

But the Queen didn't stop there. "I also bestow upon you the title of Royal Spinner so that you may continue your fine work!"

Zelda choked at this news, then thought of the fairies and smiled. "I have three cousins," Zelda suddenly announced. "May they come to the celebration?"

"So be it," granted the Queen.

Zelda laughed. "I'll make those fairies do all of my work!" she whispered. "What a clever girl I am!"

Soon the wedding day arrived. After the couple exchanged vows and the feast had begun, in walked the three fairies, wearing magnificent clothes.

"Hello, cousins," Zelda mumbled, hoping no one would notice their arrival. But everyone turned to look. The guests admired the fairies' finery, made from the most beautifully spun thread. The Prince, though, could see only their ugliness.

"Good *heavens!*" he gasped. "This is your family?"

He ran to Anita and asked, "What gave you such a broad foot?"

"Pumping the spinning wheel," she answered proudly.

Then he raced to Benita and asked, "What caused your tongue to hang out?"

"Moistening the flax," she said with a smile.

Finally he rushed to Bob. "What made your thumb so huge?"

"Winding the thread," he replied.

At that, the prince began to sob. "Never!" he cried.
"My beautiful bride must *never* go near a spinning wheel again!"

To Zelda's great delight, the prince began to beg and plead for her to be relieved of her role as Royal Spinner.

The Queen grew weary of the tantrum. "Very well!" she shouted.

Zelda's smile stretched from ear to ear. This was even better than she had planned!

"BUT," the Queen continued, "she *loves* to work. She told me so herself, again and again!"

"*Any* job," begged the Prince. "Any *other* job!"

As the Queen thought, her eyes scanned the room until they finally came to rest on Zelda's mother.

Zelda stopped smiling.

Soon after, Zelda's mother retired to a sunny island where ovens had not been invented.

Anita, Benita, and Bob offered their talents to the Queen and became her Royal Spinners. They enjoyed great fame and fortune throughout the kingdom.

And Zelda?
She was named the
Queen's Royal Baker.
The Prince offered to help,
as long as he didn't get
messy, hot, or sticky.
But, quite frankly,
Zelda was kept much
too busy to care.